Isa

Isa is a fearless and self-confident girl. She's always willing to go on new adventures. Her positive attitude and enthusiasm are contagious.

Marty

Isa's brother, the smallest member of the group, is a bit shy. He loves learning new things and his determination helps him to succeed.

Bally

He is a mixed-race whale with almond eyes and comes from grey, blue and white whale origins. He is loyal to his friends, helping them whenever he can.

Lola

She is a very brave and strong sawfish girl. Her independent spirit and natural leadership skills enable her to guide her friends out of sticky situations.

Pulpi

He is an octopus with five tentacles and the quickest and sportiest of all his friends. With his imagination and creativity, he can help in difficult moments.

Ray

He is a rainbow fish with a luminous tail that glows in dark places. He lights up deep murky depths as well as his friends' moods with his humour.

Mister Puff and his Minions

Mr. Puff is an evil balloon fish that terrorises and annoys the group of friends. Often, he is joined by his Minions, two small remora fish.

Copyright © 2020 Aquaelar Publishing (Raquel Santamaría Paredes)
First publication in Great Britain in 2020
Concept and text: Raquel Santamaría
Illustrations: Virvalle Carvallo
A CIP catalogue record for this book is available from the British Library.
FSC paper - Printed in China
ISBN: 978-1-9138470-0-5 (HB)   ISBN: 978-1-9138470-1-2 (eBook)

AQUAELAR

A place under the sea

By Raquel Santamaría
Illustrated by Virvalle Carvallo

 Aquaelar Publishing

Isa and her brother Marty are having an amazing holiday on a beautiful cruise ship.

"Marty, I'm going to go down
the highest slide."

"Wow! Nothing ever scares you, Isa!"

Isa and Marty are looking down the slippery slide.

"This-is-really-high," stutters Marty.

"Come on, let's go down together," says Isa.

Then, they look up to see a giant wave approaching the ship.

The giant wave drags Marty and Isa off the ship.
They fall into the big blue sea!

"Heeeeelp!" both shout at the top of their lungs.
"Stop! Don't leave without us!"

Suddenly, a strong whirlpool sucks them down under the water.

"Help, Isa! I'm drowning, I can't swim."

"I can't either, Marty. Quickly, give me your hand!"

The current takes them both to the bottom of the sea.

They land on a bed of beautiful coral and fall into a deep sleep.

Lola, the sawfish, spots the new arrivals.

Isa and Marty wake up. Their legs have transformed into marvellous mermaid tails.

"Ohhh! How lovely," says Isa. "I've always wanted to be a mermaid."

"Hmm... I think that I prefer my legs, sis!"

"Hello," says Lola.

"Hellooo! Are you a talking fish?" asks Marty, surprised.

"Yes! I'm Lola. Welcome to Aquaelar, the underwater world. Follow me! I'll show you around."

The three of them start exploring, but Marty has a problem
with his tail.

"Wait for me! My tail keeps
hitting my face."

"How funny! Look, you just have to relax your tail," explains Isa.

"Marty, drink this Fruup Juice! It's made from the best seaweed. It'll help you swim better," says Lola.

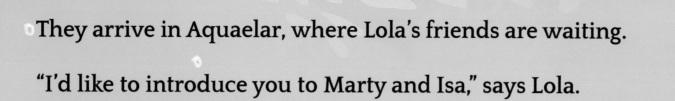

They arrive in Aquaelar, where Lola's friends are waiting.

"I'd like to introduce you to Marty and Isa," says Lola.

"Welcome! I'm Bally, a mixed-race whale."

"Hello!" says Ray, the rainbow fish. "Look at my tail, it lights up in the dark."

"I'm Pulpi. I've got five tentacles and I can swim very very fast. Now we've got two more players for our game. Yippeee!"

The new friends get ready to play a game called Tali.

"But Marty and I don't know how to play!" says Isa.

"It's easy! All you've got to do is get the ball through this ring,"
explains Bally. "Just watch Pulpi, he's the best player."

In the distance, a very angry Mr. Puff, the evil balloon fish, appears.

"Uh-oh... it's Mr. Puff! We've woken him up from his nap," says Lola.

"Let's get out of here quickly," shouts Ray. "Mr. Puff is very dangerous."

"Quick, let's hide inside this shell! I'll cover you!" whispers Bally.
"Shhhh! Don't move a muscle, otherwise he'll find us."

Mr. Puff, unable to find the hidden friends, swims away angrily.

"Phew! That was close. He almost found us," sighs Lola.
Everyone jumps for joy.
"Thank you, Bally, you saved us!"

"We really had a great time!" Isa and Marty say together.
"Let's play again tomorrow!"

AQUAELAR

Complete your collection and
have fun with their adventures under the sea

For Isabela & Martim, my niece and nephew, who inspired Isa and Marty and for Niebla, who accompanied me at the beginning of this project.

I have created Aquaelar for them and for all the children of the world.